Little Genie
Double Trouble

Little Genie
Double Trouble

MIRANDA JONES

illustrated by David Calver

SCHOLASTIC INC.

New York Toronto London Auckland Sydney
Mexico City New Delhi Hong Kong Buenos Aires

ISBN-13: 978-0-439-89631-3
ISBN-10: 0-439-89631-2

Text copyright © 2004 by Working Partners Ltd.
Illustrations copyright © 2004 by David Calver. All rights reserved.
Published by Scholastic Inc., 557 Broadway, New York, NY 10012,
by arrangement with Delacorte Press, an imprint of Bantam Doubleday
Dell Publishing Group, Inc. SCHOLASTIC and associated logos
are trademarks and/or registered trademarks of Scholastic Inc.

12 11 10 9 8 7 6 5 4 3 2 1   6 7 8 9 10 11/0

Printed in the U.S.A.   40

First Scholastic printing, November 2006

Special thanks to Narinder Dhami

Don't miss these great books!

Little Genie

Make a Wish!

Double Trouble

And coming soon:

A Puff of Pink

Castle Magic

Contents

Contents

Chapter One
Anything Can Happen in Cocoa Beach!

If you find this note, it means you are SNOOPING! Jake, if you know what's good for you, put this down RIGHT NOW! I mean it! I'm not kidding!!!

Wait a minute. What's wrong with me? I don't need to worry. My pesky little brother would never believe, not even for one second, what's been going on around here. Amazing, incredible, totally unbelievable things.

I have a genie living in my room!

Actually, she's inside an old Lava lamp Gran got me at the flea market. Little Genie was trapped inside for forty years—until I rubbed it and became her lord and master. (Hee hee!) Now I get to make real wishes. But it's not as easy as it sounds. Wishes can cause BIG problems.

And so can Little Genie!

(Even though she's cute.)

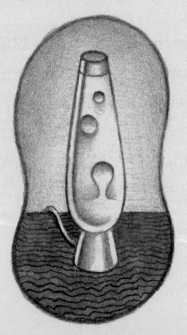

Chapter Two
Oola, Moola, Poola

"I must be dreaming," Ali Miller murmured, sitting up in bed. She rubbed her eyes and stared at her desk. Her pink furry pencil case was wiggling about as if it was alive! Suddenly, the zipper opened and a tiny head with a long blond ponytail popped out.

"Oh, Genie!" Ali said. "What *are* you doing?"

Little Genie grinned. "I thought this

would make a really cool jacket," she said, stroking the fur. "What do you think?"

Ali laughed. Having her very own genie around was definitely the most exciting thing that had ever happened to her.

"I think my pencil case would look great as a jacket, too," Ali said. "But I need it for school today."

Little Genie wriggled out of the pencil case. Her ponytail drooped. She was wearing sparkly purple pajamas and matching slippers. "I'd better put all your stuff back, then," she said with a sigh. Ali's pencils, pens, erasers, and ruler were lying on the desk in a topsy-turvy heap.

"I'll help you," Ali offered, climbing out of bed. She pulled back the curtains. Sunshine streamed into the room. "Isn't it nice out?" She yawned. "I *wish* I didn't have to go to school!" She looked hopefully over at Genie.

Little Genie held out her arm. On her wrist she wore a tiny gold watch shaped like an hourglass and filled with sparkling pink sand. "Remember what I told you," she reminded Ali. "Your second set of wishes won't start until the sand begins moving through the hourglass."

Ali nodded. She was really looking forward to her next three wishes, which would last for as long as the sand took to run from one half of the hourglass to the other. The hourglass ran on genie time, which didn't seem to follow any rules. Ali never knew how long her wishes would last, but she still couldn't *wait*. This time she was determined to wish for something she *really, really* wanted.

"Why don't you want to go to school?" asked Little Genie, heaving a ruler into the pencil case. "You sound like me. I didn't like going to Genie School either."

Ali grinned at her small friend. Little Genie had told her that she'd got into such big trouble mixing up spells that the genie teachers had expelled her. Genie had had to stay in her Lava lamp and study magic until her eleventh owner came along—who was Ali!

Genie's magic skills still weren't very reliable. Ali shook her head as she remembered her first wishes. Genie had brought a tiny purple tiger to life from a chocolate advertisement in one of Ali's magazines. The tiger had been very sweet, but keeping him hidden from Ali's mom had been a nightmare. Not to mention the ten thousand bars of chocolate that had appeared when Ali wished for her favorite treat!

"So what's happening today?" Little Genie asked, perching on Ali's strawberry-scented eraser.

Ali made a face. "A science test and drama class." Science was pretty fun. But she hated tests. And she wasn't so sure about drama. Some of the things the teacher wanted them to do were kind of dorky.

"Science and drama," Little Genie repeated longingly. "In Genie School we had to do things like blinking exercises and ponytail swinging." She frowned. "Not to mention classes like Spells for Beginners and Math for Modern Genies."

Ali twirled a pencil between her fingers. "Science is pretty cool. We do experiments and mix up chemicals in test tubes. But not today." Today she'd be trying to think of the answers to questions that were really hard.

"That sounds like Advanced Potions class!" Little Genie exclaimed. "My teacher, Miss Cauldron, didn't like me very much. She sent me back to Spells for Beginners."

"Why?" Ali asked.

"I almost singed her eyebrows off with my exploding peanut butter," Genie confessed sheepishly. "Anyway, what's drama?"

Ali shrugged. It was kind of hard to explain. "We do things like pretend to be trees." She started waving her arms about to show Little Genie what she meant and knocked the rest of the pens off the desk with her flailing hands.

"Oops!" Ali bent to pick them up.

"Drama sounds *great!*" Genie said eagerly, peering down at Ali from on top of the desk. "In Transformation we actually had to *turn* ourselves into trees,

which always seemed silly. Especially when another genie named Lampella couldn't turn herself back. Although it did make our classroom a bit more interesting." Genie smiled. "Just *pretending* to be one sounds lots more fun."

Lampella? Ali shook her head. "I don't think so."

"Well, if school's going to be such a drag, it's a shame you can't just stay home," Little Genie said. She sat on the edge of Ali's desk, swinging her legs and looking thoughtful. "Hmmm."

Suddenly, the bedroom door opened. Quick as lightning, Little Genie dived into the open pencil case, zipping it up behind her.

"Ali?" Her mom came into the room,

looking puzzled. "Who on earth were you talking to?"

Ali thought fast. Maybe this was her chance to get out of going to school! "I was just trying out my voice," she said weakly, pretending to cough. "I've got a really sore throat."

Mom raised her eyebrows. "Open up," she said.

Ali opened her mouth wide and her mom peered inside.

"It doesn't *look* red," she said briskly. "You'd better get dressed and come and have breakfast or you'll be late." She went over to the door. "Oh, and don't forget your science book," she added. "You can do some last-minute studying for your test."

Ali's shoulders sagged as her mom went out. It had been worth a try, but her mom was hard to fool.

"Help, Ali!" called a tiny voice. "I'm stuck!"

The pencil case was twitching wildly from side to side like a fluffy pink worm. Ali rushed over to the desk. Genie's pajamas had got caught in the zipper. Ali tugged gently until the pencil case opened.

"Phew!" Little Genie panted as she stuck her head out. "Thanks." She grinned at Ali. "So your mom didn't fall for it?"

"No," Ali admitted. "She never does."

Little Genie's ponytail swung back and forth. "Maybe I can help," she suggested. "After all, I can still do magic without the wishes."

"Do you think that's a good idea?" Ali asked doubtfully. She really did want to stay home, but she couldn't help thinking that Genie's magic might end up getting her into real trouble.

"Of course it's a good idea!" Little Genie cartwheeled across the desk and grinned up at Ali. "Now let me see. . . ."

She snapped her fingers, sending silver sparks shooting upward. Immediately a book appeared on the desk. It had a purple cover, and its pages were edged with silver.

"*A Genie's Big Book of Sickness Symptoms*," Ali read aloud.

Little Genie flipped open the large book and leafed through. Then her face lit up. "Ah, this should do the trick!"

she said. She pointed at Ali and began to mutter some magic words. *"Oola, moola, poola, pill, please make Ali look really ill."*

Ali waited, holding her breath. She glanced down at herself, wiggling her fingers and toes to see if anything had changed. She didn't *feel* different.

"There you are!" Genie beamed triumphantly. "Now you can stay at home today."

"But I feel exactly the same," Ali began. Then she caught a glimpse of herself in the mirror that hung over her chest of drawers. *"Genie!"* she yelled, rushing over to the mirror to take a closer look. "What have you done to me?"

Genie looked confused. "I thought you *wanted* to look sick," she said.

"Yes, but not like this!" Ali gasped. Her face was covered with enormous purple spots. "It looks like I've got a tropical disease. My mom will take me straight to the hospital if she sees me!"

"Okay." Genie shrugged. "Let's try something different, then." She flipped through the book again and began to chant another spell.

Ali anxiously watched her reflection

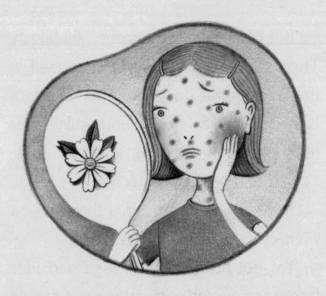

in the mirror. She breathed a sigh of relief as the bright purple spots began to fade. But then she noticed that her face was looking a bit orange. She gazed down at her hands and feet. They looked orange too. A few seconds later she was bright orange all over.

"There you go!" Genie declared, looking very pleased. "Orange fever is a very serious genie illness, you know. You're lucky you haven't got any of the other symptoms—"

"Yes, but it's not a *human* illness!" Ali interrupted her. "Genie, this isn't going to work," she groaned. She wanted to stay home and watch TV, not be rushed off to the doctor! "Make me look normal again—please!"

Little Genie frowned. "But then you'll have to go to school," she pointed out.

"That's better than looking like a giant orange!" Ali whispered loudly. As Genie muttered another spell, Ali watched her skin go back to normal. Then she turned to Genie, who was slumped beside the spell book. "Never mind, Genie," she said comfortingly. "You did your best."

"I'm sure there's other things I could have tried," Genie said with a pout, closing the book. The pink sand in her magic watch sparkled in the sunshine, catching Ali's eye. A few pink grains of sand were beginning to drift through the hourglass.

"Genie, look!" exclaimed Ali. "The sand is moving. That means my next three wishes have started!"

Genie glanced down at her watch. "Far out!" she said. "And I know *exactly* what you should wish for."

"What?" Ali asked.

"Why don't you wish for *me* to look like *you?*" Genie announced, bouncing up and down. "Then you can stay home and I can go to school in your place."

A big grin spread across Ali's face. "That's a *brilliant* idea," she said. "Let's do it quickly before my mom comes back."

Genie nodded, her ponytail bobbing. "Go on then, Ali," she urged. "Make the wish."

Ali closed her eyes. "I wish that Little Genie looked like me!" she declared.

A cloud of glittering pink smoke whirled around the room. Ali couldn't see a thing when she opened her eyes. She coughed and waited impatiently, wondering if she was going to get what she'd wished for. With Little Genie, you never quite knew!

Ali peered through the smoke as it

began to clear. Little Genie wasn't sitting on the desk anymore. She was standing on the carpet, full size like Ali. But she didn't look at all like Genie.

Instead, Ali was looking at herself!

Chapter Three
Frosty Flakes

"Oh!" Ali was so shocked, she took a step backward and sat down with a thump on the bed. It was like standing in front of a mirror. Little Genie looked *exactly* like she did, right down to her blue and white striped pajamas.

"Isn't it great?" Little Genie said. Even her voice was the same as Ali's. "Now you can have a nice day at home and I can go to school!"

"Do you really think you can pretend

to be me for a whole day?" Ali was worried. She suddenly began to wonder if this was such a good idea.

"Of course I can," Genie replied. She pushed her shoulder-length brown hair off her face, the way Ali always did, and smiled at her.

Ali smiled back. Genie sounded so confident, she had to believe her. And that meant a whole day off from school—no science test and no pretending to be a tree! She was really lucky to have her very own genie!

"Come on, Ali," Mom called up the stairs. "Hurry up or we'll be late."

"Quick, Genie." Ali grabbed a pair of jean shorts and a white shirt.

"Get dressed before my mom comes in and sees *two* of us!"

"It's not very colorful," Genie grumbled as she pulled the shirt over her head. "Can't I wear my usual clothes?"

Ali shook her head. "My friends would think I was crazy if they saw me in one of your sparkly outfits. No offense," she added, just in case Genie's feelings were hurt.

In a few minutes Genie was ready. Ali thought Genie looked perfect. She wondered if her teacher, Mrs. Jasmine, would notice.

Ali picked up her backpack and handed it to Genie. "You'd better go downstairs," she said. "I just hope you can convince Mom you're me."

"Of course I can," Genie promised, heading for the door. "She won't suspect a thing."

"And, Genie," Ali whispered, "don't do *any* spells at school!"

"Don't worry," Genie said solemnly. "I'll be careful. You know that if anyone finds out about me, I have to go back into my lamp forever."

Ali nodded. Little Genie had to be kept a complete secret. Ali hadn't even been able to tell her best friend, Mary Connolly, about her.

"Well, here goes!" Little Genie waved at Ali and skipped out of the bedroom.

Ali tiptoed after her. Little Genie looked, sounded, and acted just like her, but Ali was still nervous. Was Genie really going to be able to fool her mom? After all, she knew Ali better than anyone!

Genie bounced down the stairs, humming to herself. Ali followed her quietly and stopped about halfway down. Peering through the railings, she could just see through the kitchen door. Her heart thumped as she watched Genie walk down the hallway and into the kitchen.

Mom was sitting at the table, drinking a cup of tea while she read her newspaper. She glanced up as Genie went in. Ali waited, holding her breath.

"Hi, Mom," Genie said with a broad smile. "What's for breakfast?"

"Frosty Flakes," Mom said. "And don't take too long, honey. We're already running late." She looked at the clock. "Dad left with Jake already."

Ali let out a huge sigh of relief. Her mom hadn't noticed a thing! She really thought Genie was Ali.

Genie sat down at the table. Ali watched as she poured some Frosty Flakes into a bowl. Then she picked up her spoon and dug in. Ali groaned softly. "The milk, Genie!" she whispered, even though she knew Genie couldn't hear her.

Genie took a big mouthful of dry Frosty Flakes and immediately began to cough.

Mom looked over at her. "Are you okay?" she asked. "You shouldn't eat dry cereal."

Genie managed to swallow. She

looked around uncertainly, then picked up the big carton of orange juice that sat on the table.

"No, Genie!" Ali whispered as loudly as she dared. "We have milk with cereal— not orange juice!"

But Little Genie didn't hear. She was just about to pour the orange juice over her cereal when Ali's mom put down her newspaper. "Ali, what are you doing?" she cried, grabbing her arm. "That's orange juice, not milk."

"Oh!" Little Genie looked flustered for a moment. "Sorry, Mom. I was so busy thinking about the science test, I didn't realize."

Ali couldn't help smiling. Genie had got out of that one! Even her excuses sounded like Ali's. Meanwhile, Genie started eating. She looked a bit surprised by the loud crunching noise the cereal made. Ali guessed genies didn't normally eat Frosty Flakes.

"We'd better go," Mom said when Genie had finished. "I've got a lot to do at work today."

Ali quickly tiptoed upstairs and watched from the landing as her mom and Genie left the house. On the way out, Genie glanced back and spotted Ali. She gave her a silly grin as Ali's mom unlocked the car.

"It worked!" Ali said triumphantly. She waited until she saw the car pull away; then she got dressed in a bathing suit just for fun and went downstairs. She settled down on the sofa.

"Poor Mary," Ali said, grabbing the remote and turning on the TV. "She's got a science test while I get to watch TV!"

But there wasn't much to watch. Ali flipped through the channels until she found some cartoons. Then she switched to a music station playing a video of BoyFrenzy, her favorite band. Even more favorite since Little Genie had brought them to life from the pictures on Ali's pillow so they could sing her to sleep! Ali was singing along and copying the dance moves in the middle of the family room when suddenly the picture disappeared from the screen—and static took its place.

"Oh no!" Ali leapt up from the sofa. "What happened?" She rushed over to the TV and tried turning it off and on again, but the screen stayed fuzzy.

"Great," she groaned. "What am I going to do now?"

She glanced around the room. The sun was blazing in through the windows, but Ali didn't dare go outside in case their neighbor Mrs. Carter spotted her and wanted to know why she wasn't at school.

At least if I'd gone to school, I could have gone outside at recess with Mary, Ali thought glumly. As it was, she would be stuck inside all day.

"I think I'll go up to my bedroom and read," she decided out loud. She was just on her way upstairs when a sound at the front door made her freeze. She turned around very slowly.

Someone was standing on the doorstep.

Ali could make out a blurry shape through the door's glass panes. Was it the mailman? If she kept very quiet, perhaps he would just go away.

But then she heard the sound of a key in the lock.

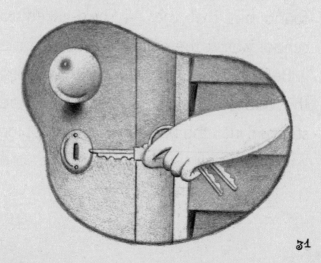

Chapter Four
Stuck Indoors

"Noooo!" Ali cried, panicked. Had her mom come back home? Maybe she'd forgotten something. Or maybe she'd found out that the Ali she'd taken to school wasn't the *real* Ali!

Before Ali could turn and run upstairs, the door was pushed open. A woman stepped into the hall, carrying a shopping bag.

Ali gasped. "Gran!"

Gran took off her sunglasses, looking just as surprised to see Ali. As usual, she was flamboyantly dressed. She wore a Hawaiian-print yellow shirt and striped pants. "Ali! What are you doing here?"

Ali opened and closed her mouth. *Think!* she ordered herself. "Well, Mrs. Jasmine said I could come home to change my clothes," she babbled. "I spilled paint on myself in class this morning."

"You came home by yourself?"

"It was a lot of paint," Ali fibbed, trying to look normal.

"Oh." Gran stared at Ali's bathing suit. "Are you wearing that to school?"

Ali said the first thing that came into her head. "I couldn't find any clean T-shirts."

"Can I help you look?" Gran offered.

"No, that's okay," Ali said quickly. "I think I know where Mom put them." She took a deep breath. "Anyway, what are *you* doing here, Gran?"

"I popped over to drop this off for your mom." Gran reached into the bag and pulled out a brightly patterned lamp shade. "I bought it at the thrift shop. I thought it would look really nice in your living room. Give it a bit of color."

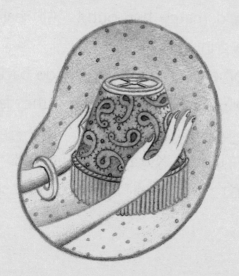

Ali couldn't help laughing. She called her gran the Junk Queen because she loved finding bargains at garage sales and flea markets. Sometimes Ali liked the stuff her gran bought, but her mom was less enthusiastic. And the lamp shade was a million miles from anything Ali's mom would choose. It was made of orange and purple satin, with long pink fringe. Ali could just imagine her mom's face when she saw it. Genie would probably love it. It would match her outfits, Ali realized with a grin.

"Come on, I'll give you a ride back to school," said Gran, putting the lamp shade on the hall table.

Ali gulped. "Okay," she agreed. She couldn't very well say no! She sped upstairs and changed into her clothes. This was all going wrong! What would everyone at school say if *two* Alis turned up? She'd just have to hope no one spotted her before she could sneak back home.

As Gran drove them down the road in her battered little car, Ali began to feel more and more worried. When they reached Montgomery Elementary School, she slumped down in her seat so she couldn't be seen through the window.

"Sit up, Ali," said her gran, pulling alongside the playground. "You'll give yourself a bad back. Here we are."

"Thanks, Gran." Ali took a quick look out the car window. Thank goodness it wasn't recess, she thought. Everyone was inside. But there was always a chance that someone might look out and see her.

"Have a nice day!" Gran called as Ali climbed from the car. Luckily, she didn't wait for Ali go inside. She just drove off with a toot of her horn.

Ali breathed a sigh of relief. "Okay," she mumbled. "Time to walk back home again." At least she didn't live too far away. Before she set off, though, she couldn't resist peeking in her classroom window. There was Little Genie, sitting in Ali's place by the window, next to Mary. Even though she knew Genie had taken her place, Ali still got a shock at seeing someone who looked *exactly* like her sitting in her seat! It felt very strange.

Little Genie had her head down and was scribbling away like mad. Ali guessed that the class was in the middle of the science test. She wondered how Genie would do. She was sure Genie knew even less about science than she did! Maybe Genie would use magic, Ali thought as she hurried off down the street. She'd told Genie not to use magic at school, but it might be worth it if it meant Ali got a good grade on the test. And maybe Mrs. Jasmine would get a nice surprise when she marked Ali's paper!

Ali arrived back home feeling hot and tired. She couldn't wait to get inside and have a cool drink. But when she reached the front gate, she had to dodge behind a tree to hide from Mrs. Carter, who was coming out of her house with a shopping bag over one arm. Ali held her breath and stood very still until she heard Mrs. Carter walk off in the opposite direction.

"This is too much," Ali said gloomily as she finally let herself into the cool, air-conditioned house. Her wish to have Little Genie take her place at school had seemed like a good idea at the time, but as usual with genie magic, things weren't as simple as they seemed! And Ali wasn't looking forward to a stuffy afternoon stuck indoors with no TV. She decided to make some lunch to cheer herself up.

Ali went into the kitchen and poured herself a glass of lemonade. Suddenly, there was a flash of pink smoke and a loud bang! Ali nearly jumped out of her skin. The smoke cleared quickly, and there was Genie, beaming, and still looking exactly like Ali.

"Genie!" Ali gasped. "Please don't do that!"

"Do what? Oh, that. It's the best way to travel, you know. And I've been having a great time!" Genie exclaimed. "Have you enjoyed yourself too?" Then she looked closer at Ali. "Hey, you changed out of your pajamas and you're sweating. You haven't been outside, have you?"

Ali explained how Gran had turned up unexpectedly. "The TV's not working, I can't go outside, and I'm really bored," she finished grumpily. "Anyway, what are you doing here? You're supposed to stay at school for lunch."

"I know," Genie said. "But I wanted to come home and tell you all the great things I've been doing."

"Like what?" Ali asked, feeling a bit jealous. It sounded like Genie had been having a much better time than she had!

"Well, we had that science test," Genie began. "And it was easy peasy!"

Ali frowned. "What do you mean?"

"Mrs. Jasmine said it was a multiple-choice test," Genie explained. "You had lots of different answers to choose from, and you had to check the right box."

"And you thought that was easy?" Ali asked doubtfully. She always thought that having more than one answer to a question just made it harder to know which one was right!

Genie nodded her head vigorously. "Oh *yes*," she said. "I checked *all* the boxes, so I *know* I got the right answer every time. Mrs. Jasmine corrected the papers just before lunch, and she's so pleased, she wants to see you every night after school next week!"

Ali groaned. Genie had really got her into trouble this time. Mrs. Jasmine must have thought she wasn't taking the test seriously, and now she'd got a week of detention! "How do you like Mary?" she asked, feeling even more jealous.

"She's hep," Genie said breezily. "But she keeps looking at me in this really funny way. Like this." She glanced sideways at Ali with such a big frown that she was almost cross-eyed.

"You haven't done anything to make her suspicious, have you?" Ali demanded.

"Of course not," Genie said. "Everyone believed that I was you. Even this girl with long blond hair that I don't think likes you very much. She looked at me like I was a bad smell or something!" Genie sounded very indignant.

Ali nodded. "That's Tiffany Andrews." Tiffany was the class snob. Her family was rich. She was always bragging about all the things they bought her. And she seemed to think that Ali and Mary weren't good enough to be her friends—not that Ali and Mary wanted to be her friends in the first place.

"Well, I'd better be going." Little Genie beamed at Ali. "I'm really looking forward to drama. See you later!" She held up her hand, ready to snap her fingers and make herself disappear.

"Wait, don't go yet," Ali said quickly. She stared at the hourglass watch on Genie's wrist. Genie had turned it around so that the hourglass part was hidden on the inside of her wrist. Hardly any sand had trickled through. "I've still got two wishes left. There must be something I can wish for to make my afternoon a bit more fun."

Genie thought for a minute. Then her face lit up. "Hey, why don't you use your second wish to make yourself tiny?" she suggested. "I could take you to school with me in my backpack!"

"That's a great idea!" Ali could listen to the teacher, but she wouldn't have to *do* anything embarrassing! She took a deep breath.

"My second wish is, I wish I was tiny!" she said.

Chapter Five
Traveling Genie Style

As soon as she made her wish, Ali began to feel dizzy. The room spun and she closed her eyes, feeling a bit sick.

"Ali?" Genie's voice suddenly sounded very loud. "Where are you?"

Cautiously Ali opened her eyes. She was standing next to a huge, shiny tree trunk. Then she took a closer look. It was the leg of the kitchen table. She really *had* shrunk!

"I'm down here," Ali called. Her voice sounded tiny too. She stared up at Little

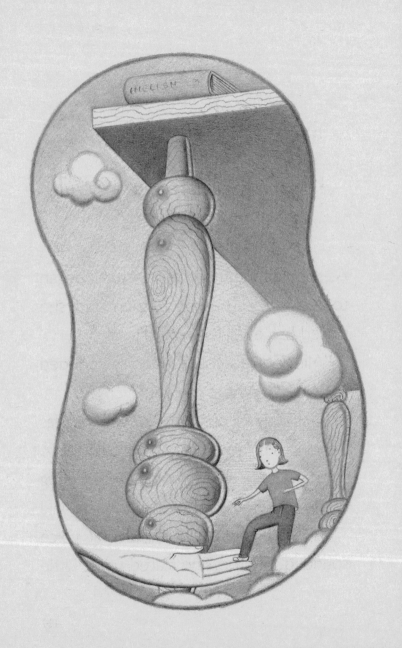

Genie, whose face loomed over her. "This is really weird."

Little Genie laughed. "You'll get used to it," she promised. "After all, I'm that size most of the time." She bent down and carefully picked Ali up. "Don't worry, I'll look after you."

She put Ali down on the table while she retrieved her backpack. Ali stared at the pepper grinder next to her. She wasn't much bigger than that! She hoped it didn't fall on her—it looked heavy.

"You'll be quite safe in here," Little Genie said, unzipping one of the backpack pockets. "You'll be able to see and hear everything that's going on."

She slid Ali gently into the pocket. Ali ducked her head through the zipper and looked around. At the bottom there were a bunch of empty candy wrappers, paper clips, old papers, and some sticky pieces of grime. It was about time she cleaned her backpack, she thought, wrinkling her nose.

"Okay, Ali," she heard Little Genie say. "We're off now. Hold tight!"

The pocket was zipped up, and Ali was plunged into darkness. She felt the backpack being lifted off the table, and then there was a loud fizzing noise followed by a *whoosh!*

Ali's heart thumped with excitement. This was traveling Genie style! The backpack began to bounce all over the place, and Ali clung to a pencil to stop herself from being thrown around too much. She began to feel sick all over again. She crouched down and hugged her knees, hoping they'd get to school very soon.

There was a bang, and the backpack came to a stop. A tiny wisp of pink smoke drifted through the pocket.

"We're here," whispered Genie.

There was the sound of the zipper

being undone, and then bright daylight flooded into the pocket. Ali jumped to her feet. Blinking, she carefully popped her head out. They were in the school playground, behind one of the oak trees at the edge. The playground was full of kids.

"Genie!" Ali groaned. "What if someone had *seen* us?" How on earth would Genie, looking like Ali, have explained arriving in a puff of glittering pink smoke?

"Don't fuss," Genie told her. "No one's noticed a thing. Come on, let's go and find everyone."

Ali watched from the half-open pocket as Genie walked across the playground. It was very strange to see everyone looking so huge while she was so small. She couldn't see Mary anywhere, but Tiffany Andrews was shooting hoops with her friends. As usual, she spent most of the time bossing them around and shouting at everyone who got in her way.

"Hey, that looks like fun!" Genie said as Tiffany took a shot at the hoop. "I bet I could do that."

Ali shook her head fiercely. "No way! Tiffany and her friends always get to the basketball court first," she said through clenched teeth. "And they never let anyone else play with them."

To Ali's alarm, she suddenly noticed that Tiffany was walking toward them, glaring at Genie. Quickly she ducked down inside the empty pocket.

"What are you looking at, Ali?" Tiffany

demanded. "I suppose you want to show us how good you are at hoops!"

Tiffany's friends laughed.

Ali had to bite her lip to stop herself from replying crossly that she *was* good at basketball.

"Well, yes," Ali heard Genie say cheerfully. "Thanks." Ali felt Genie slip the backpack off her shoulder and put it on the ground.

"No, Genie!" Ali whispered in a panic. "Tiffany wasn't *really* asking you to play!" What would all her friends think if they saw her shooting hoops with Tiffany Andrews? But when Ali popped her head out of the pocket, she was just in time to see Genie grab the ball from Tiffany and aim a shot at the hoop at the far end of the court.

"You'll never score from there," Tiffany scoffed as the ball sailed through the air. "You're too far away."

Genie shrugged. "We'll see," she said.

Everyone stopped and watched as the ball flew in a graceful arc toward the hoop. It fell straight through the net and bounced onto the court.

Tiffany's face was red. "That was just a fluke," she snapped. "You couldn't do it again."

"Sure I could," Genie said, sounding surprised. "It was easy!"

Ali couldn't help laughing at the sight of Tiffany's outraged expression.

"I could show you how I did it if you like," Genie offered. She looked down at Ali in the backpack and winked. "Look," she instructed Tiffany, speaking very slowly. "You hold the ball like this. . . ."

Ali winced. Genie was being quite funny, but Tiffany was getting really mad. Ali was sure Tiffany would try to pay her back sometime. And knowing Ali's luck, that would be when her wish was over and she was back at school as herself!

"Genie, stop it!" Ali whispered as loudly as she dared, but Genie didn't hear her.

"Ali?"

Ali jumped when she heard Mary's voice behind them.

"What are you doing?" Mary asked, looking very surprised. "You're not playing basketball with *Tiffany Andrews,* are you?"

"Not exactly," Genie said, grinning broadly as Tiffany flounced off across the court with her friends. "I offered to give her some lessons, but she said no."

Ali peered out and saw Mary give Genie a very strange look. "Are you okay?" Mary asked. "You've been kind of weird today."

Ali squeezed her eyes shut. Mary was obviously getting very suspicious.

"I'm fine," Genie said breezily. "Never felt better."

"And where did you go at lunch?" Mary went on. "I saved a seat for you but you didn't show up."

"I—I had to go to the office," Genie stammered.

"Why?" Mary wanted to know.

"Well, I—I forgot my math book."

"But we don't have math this afternoon," Mary pointed out, looking more confused than ever. "We've got drama."

Genie shrugged. "Oh, well, at least I'll have it ready for tomorrow!"

Ali was beginning to feel a bit anxious. What if Mary didn't want to be friends with her anymore because Genie was being so weird? She had to tell Mary what was going on. Without thinking, Ali waved at her friend. "Mary! Over here!" she called in her tiny voice.

Genie glanced down and frowned. Quick as a flash, she zipped the pocket right up. Ali had to duck out of the way to stop herself from being caught in the zipper as it whizzed shut.

"Genie, let me out!" she yelled. But Genie ignored her.

Ali sat down on a scrunched-up candy wrapper, feeling fed up. She knew she shouldn't have tried to attract Mary's attention. She'd only done it because she didn't want to lose her best friend. "But if I told Mary everything, Genie would have to go back into the lamp. And then I wouldn't be able to have any more wishes," Ali mumbled. Although looking at how the wishes had turned out so far, maybe they weren't worth all the trouble!

Chapter Six
A Huge Storm

When the bell rang, Ali felt the backpack swing up into the air. She bounced around as Genie walked. At last the backpack was put down with a thud, and the zipper opened.

"Where are we, Genie?" whispered Ali. She could hear a lot of voices. "In the classroom?" She was too nervous to pop her head out and look.

"No, we're in the hall," Genie told her,

bending down low. "We're about to start drama class. I can't wait! Sorry for zipping you up like that. But I couldn't let you tell Mary!"

"Are you talking to your backpack?" Ali peeked out with one eye and saw Mary standing there, staring at Genie.

"Who, me?" Genie joked. "No way! I was just talking to myself."

Ali was very relieved when Mary burst out laughing. "Oh, that's all right then. That's completely normal!" she teased.

"Okay, people." Ali's drama teacher, Mrs. Harvey, clapped as they filed into the large room that was used for drama as well as gym class. "Get into groups of five, please."

Little Genie propped the backpack

against the wall so Ali would have a good view of all the action. Then Mary grabbed her hand, and they ran into the center of the room.

Ali watched as the class began to divide itself up with a lot of noise and bustle. Genie and Mary were in the same group, but there were six of them, and only four in Tiffany Andrews's group.

"Ali, will you join that group, please?" Mrs. Harvey called, pointing to Tiffany and her friends.

Bad luck, Genie, Ali thought as she saw Tiffany and her friends making faces at each other. Genie didn't look bothered, though. She bounced across the room to join the other group, ignoring their glares.

"Today we're going to imagine that we're at sea and a huge storm has blown up," Mrs. Harvey told the class. "Imagine what it would be like to be tossed around on the waves with the rain beating down and a gale-force wind blowing in your faces, sea spray everywhere."

"Can we pretend to be seasick?" asked a round-faced boy with messy brown hair.

Ali rolled her eyes. Barry Oakes always thought he was *so* funny.

Mrs. Harvey sighed. "If you must."

The teacher put some classical music on the CD player, and the groups began to shuffle around. At first the music was quiet, although it sounded very loud to Ali's tiny ears. Then, with a couple of drumrolls, the music grew louder and louder. It was a good thing Genie hadn't put the backpack next to the CD player, Ali thought. It would have deafened her!

The groups were now staggering around the room, clinging to each other and wiping imaginary water from their faces. Ali had to admit that it *did* look like fun. And Genie was pretty good! She swayed from side to side, lurching about and pretending to clutch at ropes.

"Watch out, crew!" Genie shouted as she slid across the floor and bumped into Tiffany, who looked furious. "The storm's really blowing up now!"

Grinning, Ali leaned farther out of the backpack to get a better look. But as she did so, a barrette slipped out and landed on the floor.

"Oh no!" Ali bit her lip. The barrette, which had a little strawberry on the end, was one of her favorites. And the way everyone was running around the room, it was going to get stepped on any minute now. Barry Oakes had nearly squashed it already with his huge sneakers.

Ali quickly made up her mind to do something. She heaved herself out of the

pocket and scrambled down the side of the backpack. Just as she stretched out her hand to pick up the barrette, Barry lumbered past. He kicked the barrette without even noticing. It flew across the floor and landed even farther away, near Genie's group.

"Oh no," Ali groaned. She would have to make a dash for it right to the other side of the room, avoiding all those enormous prancing feet—while making sure no one saw her!

Hugging the wall, Ali ran as fast as she could to the barrette. She hid behind a pile of gym mats to catch her breath. *Phew! What's that awful smell?* she wondered. She looked over and saw an old gym sock lying in a smelly heap beside her. Yuck! Pinching her nose, Ali raced out into the middle of the room. Luckily everyone was too busy in their storm-tossed boats to notice her. Even Little Genie!

As Ali bent to pick up the barrette, she saw Tiffany glance over at Mrs. Harvey. The teacher was talking to another group and had her back to the students. Tiffany grinned nastily and gave Genie an enormous push. Genie gasped and went sprawling on the floor.

Tiffany laughed. "Someone's fallen overboard, and we don't have any life jackets!"

Ali glared at her. "Genie, are you all right?" she called in her tiny voice. But there was so much noise in the room, Genie couldn't hear her.

Genie jumped up, rubbing her elbow. "No problem, everybody!" she shouted cheerfully. "It's a good thing I can swim!"

That'll show Tiffany! thought Ali. She watched as Genie zoomed across the room toward Barry's group.

"Help!" Genie yelled, waving madly at Barry. "Can I come on board?"

"I thought you said you could swim," Barry called.

"I can," Genie replied, dog-paddling. "But this water's freezing!"

"Come on in, then," Barry said with a grin.

"You know what?" Genie said as Barry grabbed her hand to haul her into the pretend boat. "It'd be a lot more fun if there was a *real* storm!"

Ali's heart began to pound. What was Little Genie planning now? "No, Genie!" she yelled.

But her words were swept away by a sudden gust of wind that seemed to come from nowhere. It raged around the room, rattling the windows and making it impossible to hear anything except Tiffany Andrews's shrieking.

Ali tried to run across the room to the

safety of the backpack, but the wind was too strong. She clung to a nearby chair leg, wondering what was going to happen next. Somehow she didn't think Genie's idea of a real storm would stop at a gust of wind.

And then Ali saw a huge green-blue wave of water rising slowly at the far end of the room. It loomed higher and higher until it had covered the windows!

"Oh no!" Ali gasped.

Mrs. Harvey was staring at it open-mouthed. So was everyone else.

"Man the lifeboats!" yelled Genie, rushing around with a big grin on her face. "Wave ahoy!"

And then, very slowly, the wall of water rolled over. It crashed to the floor, rushing toward every corner of the room. The noise was deafening.

Mrs. Harvey raced over to the door and pulled it open, waving desperately for the class to run outside. Ali wanted to follow, but she was too scared of getting trampled. There was nothing she could do, so, feeling very scared, she stayed under the chair. And when she looked up, the huge wave was plunging straight toward her.

Chapter Seven
Another Genie

"Help!" Ali yelled, cowering under the chair. She was already wet through from the spray. In just a moment, the water would be right over her head.

"Ali!"

Above the roar of the water, Ali heard someone shout her name. Footsteps splashed across the room, and suddenly there was a very damp Genie, still looking like Ali, kneeling beside the chair. Ali

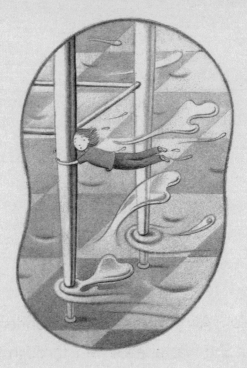

had never been so glad to see anyone in her life!

"Come on!" Genie said urgently, lifting Ali up.

"Ali!" Mrs. Harvey called anxiously from the door. The rest of the class were standing shivering in the corridor. "Over here!"

Ali glanced over just in time to see the teacher jump out of the way as the water crashed into the doorway.

"Genie!" Ali shouted. "Look! The door is flooded. We won't be able to get out!"

But Genie had a plan. Clutching Ali in her hand, she sprinted to the other end of the room just ahead of the rolling wave. Genie grabbed Ali's backpack off the floor, then jumped onto the piano stool and climbed right up on top of the piano. The wave smashed against the wall, sending a spray of water over them. Ali gulped as she pushed her wet hair out of her eyes and gazed down at the choppy water swirling on the floor below.

"You saved my life!" Ali gasped. "Thanks, Genie."

"It was lucky I spotted you," Genie said. A drop of water slid down her cheek. She helped Ali into the backpack pocket and zipped it half shut. "I didn't know the storm was going to be this big!" she confessed. "That wave was gnarly!" Then she winked at Ali, her eyes sparkling with mischief. "It's been fun, though, hasn't it?"

The wind was still thundering around the room, and the waves were still sweeping up and down. Suddenly a loud siren could be heard above the howling wind.

"Listen," Ali said through chattering teeth. "It's the fire department!" The rest of her class, who were standing just outside the door, started to cheer.

A few moments later a group of fire-fighters in yellow helmets and big boots appeared in the doorway. One of them waded over to Genie and Ali. "Come on," he said. "Let's get you out of here."

Genie clutched the backpack tightly as the firefighter picked her up and waded back across the hall. Ali couldn't resist peeking out to see what was going on. The water had flooded down the corridor and into some classrooms. The whole school had been sent outside to line up in the playground, just like a fire drill. Everyone from Mrs. Harvey's class was wet and shivering, and Ali could hear Tiffany Andrews being a drama queen as usual, moaning and complaining at the top of her voice.

"I bet my bag's ruined!" she was protesting. "I had to leave it behind. And it cost a lot!"

Meanwhile, Mrs. Harvey was talking to one of the firefighters. She looked very pale.

"We think a water main must have burst," the firefighter said. "I've never seen so much water."

Mrs. Harvey nodded. "Yes, that must be what happened." She turned to her class. "Mrs. Jasmine and I will be phoning your parents to come for an early dismissal so that you can go home and dry off. If we can't reach your parents, we'll call your emergency pickup number."

Ali shivered. That meant Gran would be coming to get her.

Mary squelched over to Genie. "Hey, Ali, wasn't that *cool?*" She was soaking wet, but she was grinning like crazy. "Scary, but fun! It was just like being in a real storm!"

"I know!" Genie agreed, squeezing some water from her hair. "I can't believe a water main burst just as we were acting out that storm scene!" She glanced down at Ali and winked.

Inside the backpack pocket Ali was freezing. She tried wrapping one of the empty gum wrappers around her to warm up, but it didn't help. All she wanted to do was go home, climb into a steaming bath, and have a hot drink.

"There's your grandma, Ali," Mary said.

"Oh." Genie sounded puzzled. Ali

watched as Genie looked at the cars pulling up outside the school gate. "Um, where, exactly?"

Ali groaned. Of course Genie didn't know who Gran was! Even though Gran had bought the Lava lamp for Ali, Genie hadn't appeared until Ali had started polishing the lamp at home.

"*There,*" said Mary, pointing. "Have you still got water in your eyes or something?" Ali saw Mary giving Genie a strange look. "That's her car, isn't it?"

"Oh, *that* Gran," Genie said breezily. "I didn't know who you meant at first."

Ali could see from the look on Mary's face that she definitely thought there was something seriously wrong with her friend! "I'm going to have a lot of explaining to do," Ali mumbled, shaking her head.

"Are you two all right?" Gran was hurrying across the playground toward Genie and Mary. "What an awful thing to happen. You're soaked through."

"We're fine, Gran," Genie said.

"Mary, can we give you a ride home?" Gran offered.

"Thanks! I'll tell Mrs. Harvey," Mary said.

As soon as Mrs. Harvey said it was okay, Gran hurried them over to the car and put the heater on full blast. Ali was dying to pop her head out of the backpack to dry her hair, but she didn't dare.

They dropped Mary off, and then Gran drove straight to the Millers' house.

"Now go upstairs and get out of those wet clothes," she told Genie, taking the backpack from her and putting it down in the hall. "I'll run you a bath and make you some hot chocolate. That'll soon warm you up."

"Maybe I should unpack my backpack first," Genie began. "My papers might be wet—"

"That can wait," Gran said firmly. "Off you go."

Ali's face fell as she heard Genie and Gran going upstairs. She needed a bath and a cup of hot chocolate too! She couldn't unzip the pocket without Genie. She was stuck.

It seemed like ages until she heard Genie coming downstairs again.

"Gran, is it all right if I take my hot chocolate upstairs and start my homework?" Genie asked.

"Of course," Gran said, much to Ali's relief.

Ali felt the backpack being lifted into the air. She bounced and bobbed from side to side as Genie ran upstairs. When the zipper was pulled open, Ali scrambled out onto her bed.

"Are you okay?" Genie asked. She looked very warm and snug in Ali's favorite sweats.

"N-no," Ali stammered through clattering teeth. *"Aschoo!"*

"How can we warm you up?" Genie wondered. "You're too small to go into the bath. You might slip down the drain!

And you're too tiny to fit into any of your other clothes. We could wrap you in a sock or something."

"No, I know what to do," Ali said, sneezing again. She was so cold, she was ready to try desperate measures. "I want my third wish. I wish for something to make me warm and dry."

Genie clapped. "I know just the thing," she said excitedly. "My friend Ray will do the trick! I knew him at Genie School."

"No, Genie," Ali gasped. "Not *another* genie." One was more than enough!

But it was too late. Genie had already snapped her fingers and was frowning in concentration as she cast her spell.

Chapter Eight
The Ro-20

Ali's bedroom windows flew open and cold air streamed in.

"Genie, you're supposed to be warm-ing me up," Ali complained, trying to pull her quilt around her. "Close the win-dows!"

"Just a minute." Genie ran over to the window and peered out. "Oh, look! Here's Ray."

Ali watched in amazement as a puff of

bright yellow smoke whirled into the room. With a loud *whoosh!*, something that looked the same size and shape as Ali's bedside rug swept through the window and skidded to a halt above Ali's desk. It was a flying carpet, golden yellow with orange and red stripes!

Sitting cross-legged on the carpet was a round-faced, smiling genie. He wore a gold vest, an orange hat, and baggy yellow pants. In his arms he carried something wrapped in a silky golden cloth.

"Ray!" Genie waved in delight. "It's been ages since I've seen you."

"Hi, Genie," Ray called down, peering over the edge of the carpet. "Is it okay to land?"

"Sure, go ahead," Genie said.

Ali stared as Ray guided the carpet
down from the ceiling. It settled lightly on
the floor and Ray stood up, revealing
dazzling slippers with long, curled-over
toes. He was taller than Genie, and very
tan.

"This is Ali, my lord and master," Genie

said excitedly, pointing to Ali on the bed. "Ali, this is Ray, an old friend of mine. He sells flying carpets."

"I'm very pleased to meet you, Ali," Ray said cheerily, bowing low with an elegant wave of his hand. "I am honored indeed to meet Little Genie's lord and master." He glanced at Genie with a grin. "There were times at Genie School when even her closest friends doubted that this happy day would come!"

"Hi," Ali said, still shivering. Was this really what she had wished for? She didn't have a clue how Ray was going to warm her up!

"Ray was the coolest cat in class when we were learning how to fly magic carpets," Genie explained. "I was *hopeless*. I kept crashing, and in the end our teacher, Mr. Abracadabra, would only let me use a doormat."

Ray proudly tapped his carpet with his toe. "I'm flying the latest model now," he told her. "This is the R-60, the most expensive carpet I have in the shop. Top speed 140 miles per hour, and it never overturns, not even in the strongest wind."

"Really?" Genie looked very impressed and bent down to stroke the gold fringe.

Ray yawned hugely. "Sorry," he apologized. "I was refueling in the Sahara when you called, and I've got jet lag. What did you want me for, Genie?"

Quickly Genie explained what had happened.

"In that case, ladies, it's lucky I've brought my sunlamp." With a flourish, Ray unwrapped the object in his arms. It looked a bit like the reading lamp on Ali's desk, except that it was a shiny golden color. Ray put it down on the desk and pointed it in Ali's direction.

"A sunlamp?" Ali said. "Well, that seems like a good idea."

"This will warm you up in no time," Ray promised.

"You can plug it in under the desk," Ali said, feeling another giant sneeze tickling her nose. She hoped he would hurry up.

Ray shook his head. "It doesn't need to be plugged in," he said, waving his hand in front of the lamp. "It's magic!"

"Like my Lava lamp," Genie added. She

sat cross-legged on Ray's carpet and smiled encouragingly at Ali.

Ali watched as the giant lightbulb inside the lamp began to glow. The light was very bright, but soon Ali felt a deliciously warm beam coming from it. She lay down on the bed and shut her eyes as the heat soaked into her and dried her clothes.

"So how's the flying carpet business these days, Ray?" Genie asked.

"Not bad at all," answered Ray. "I sell a lot of these R-60s. It doesn't just go up and down, you know. Oh no, you've got 360-degree movement, and it can even do loop-the-loops. You have to hang on tight, though."

"That's bookin'!" Genie said. She

turned to Ali. "How are you feeling?"

"Great," Ali replied with her eyes still closed. "It's like I'm lying on a beach!" She opened her eyes and sat up. She was warm and dry all over. "Thanks very much," she said, grinning at Ray.

"No problem," he said, giving her another sweeping bow.

"You can turn the lamp off now, if you like," Ali added.

"Actually, the lamp's part of your wish, so it has to stay on until all the sand runs through the hourglass," Genie explained cheerfully. "Ray has to stay too."

Ali's heart sank. She'd managed to keep one genie hidden from her family so far, but it was going to be much more difficult with two!

Just then she heard the front door open and close downstairs. There was the sound of voices in the hall.

"That's Dad talking to Gran," Ali gasped. "He just got home from work. Genie, you'd better go downstairs." Her tummy rumbled loudly, and she realized she hadn't had anything to eat since breakfast. "And would you bring me something to eat?"

"Sure," Genie promised. "Just give me five minutes." She hurried over to the door and went downstairs.

Ray yawned again. "Do you mind if I have a nap?" he asked Ali. "I'm really tired."

Ali shook her head. "Of course not." She scrambled down the quilt onto the floor and went over to look at Ray's carpet. A pattern of round yellow suns was woven along the orange and red stripes, and the soft, floaty fringes were made of gold thread. "Is it very difficult to learn how to fly a carpet?" Ali asked curiously.

"Not really," Ray replied. "You just have to practice. I could give you a great deal, if you like." He frowned thoughtfully. "If you're a beginner, I'd recommend the R-20. It comes in red or green, fringe extra, and it's guaranteed for a hundred hours of flying time. It doesn't do loop-the-loops, so you'll be quite safe. Just keep away from trees and tall buildings while you're practicing."

For a moment Ali was tempted. Her

own flying carpet! It would be great. "Well . . . ," she began.

"Okay, you've twisted my arm," Ray said quickly. "Seeing as you're a friend of Little Genie's, I can give you fifty percent off. Only fifteen gold coins. That's a real bargain."

Reluctantly Ali shook her head. "I'd *never* be able to keep it a secret from my family," she said. "People around here just don't have flying carpets."

Ray's eyes gleamed. "Really? Maybe I should think about opening a shop!"

Ali laughed. Having a shop selling flying carpets in Cocoa Beach would be great! She bet Tiffany Andrews could talk her parents into getting her an R-60 in no time.

Ray yawned again. "On the other hand, I'm not sure I like the weather here too much. Let me know if you change your mind," he said, curling up on the carpet. "You won't get a better deal than that on the R-20." And in five minutes he was fast asleep.

Ali admired the patterns on his carpet for a bit longer. Then she glanced at the door. Where was Little Genie? She was *starving*.

Half an hour passed. Then an hour. Ali was still hungry, and there was no sign of Little Genie. Ray was still asleep, but every now and then he muttered things like, *"The R-40's a good family model, plenty of space for the kids; it's even got a Snakes and Ladders board woven into the pattern to keep them quiet on those long journeys. . . ."*

Ali started to feel very bored. She was too small to read a book or put some music on her CD player. Ray's lamp was still shining brightly on her desk, and the room was beginning to feel uncomfortably warm. She had just decided to have a nap to forget about her rumbling tummy when she heard footsteps coming up the stairs.

"Sorry I took so long," Little Genie puffed, bursting into the room. "We all ate dinner, and then I offered to dry all the dishes so Jake could have some playtime. He told me it was my turn."

"What?" Ali said, frowning. "That's not true!"

Genie shrugged. "After that, your dad and Jake did homework, and since I didn't have any, your mom and Gran and I watched this TV show about these people who live on the same street who keep having arguments with each other."

"That's *Sunshine Street*," Ali sighed. It was her favorite show, and now she'd missed it. Then a thought struck her. "But isn't the TV broken?"

"Your mom fixed it," Genie said. "She said it was the fuse. Anyway, look." She held out a plate. "I brought you a cheese sandwich."

Ali was too small to hold the whole sandwich, so Genie broke off a tiny corner and handed it to her. By the time Ali had finished the piece, she was full!

"Ray can finish the rest," Genie said. She yawned. "I think I'll go to bed."

"You won't be able to get into your lamp, though, will you?" Ali pointed out. "Not while you're being me."

"That's okay," Genie said. "I can sleep in your bed."

"But what about me?" Ali asked. She glanced over at Genie's Lava lamp on her desk. "Hey, can I sleep in there?"

"No, sorry," Genie apologized. "You don't have the right magic to get into my lamp. But you can sleep on my—sorry, *your*—pillow, if you like."

"Okay," Ali said, feeling a bit disappointed. She'd been looking forward to seeing what was inside Genie's lamp!

Ali settled down on the pillow.

Meanwhile, Genie put on a pair of Ali's pajamas.

"What are we going to do about *that?*" said Ali, pointing at Ray's lamp. It was dark outside now, and the glow seemed even brighter. "Can't we wrap it up in something?"

"That won't work," Genie muttered sleepily, getting into bed and snuggling down. "It's a magic lamp. You can't stop it once it's shining."

Ali looked down at Ray, who was still curled up on his carpet. The light didn't seem to be bothering him at all—he was obviously used to it!

"But how are we going to get to sleep?" Ali grumbled, squinting.

Genie mumbled something, and then

she began to snore very gently. She was asleep already, Ali thought glumly. She jumped as Genie rolled over. If she wasn't careful, Genie might squash her!

Ali curled up in a ball and put her hands over her eyes. She was just drifting off to sleep when footsteps on the landing made her jump so she almost fell off the pillow. Genie woke too and sat up, blinking and yawning.

"Ali?" Mom called from downstairs. She sounded annoyed. "It's really late. Why have you still got your light on?"

Chapter Nine
Sunglasses at Night

Ali gasped. "Quick, Genie, do something."

"S-sorry, Mom," Genie stammered. She was still half asleep and rubbing her eyes. "I just had to put the light on to, um, do something?"

"What?" Mom asked.

"I can't remember." Genie yawned.

The light of Ray's lamp was shining under the gap at the bottom of the bedroom door. Ali's sweatpants were lying across the bottom of the bed where Genie had left them. Quickly Ali scrambled across the quilt. Her feet sank in with every step. It felt like she was walking across a giant snow-drift! Grabbing the sweatpants' waist-band string, she climbed down to the floor as if she was climbing down a rope in the school gym. Puffing and panting, she pulled and pulled until finally the sweatpants slithered onto the floor with a soft thud. Then she started dragging them toward the door.

"Genie!" she called. "I need a hand! We can use my sweatpants to block out the light under the door."

Yawning, Genie scrambled out of bed to help her. Together they pushed the sweatpants tightly against the gap at bottom of the door. Now Ray's lamp wouldn't shine onto the landing.

"I've turned my light off now," Genie called.

"Good," Mom called back. "Now get some sleep. Good night."

Ali and Genie both sighed with relief. "That was close!" Genie breathed.

"But I think the light's getting even brighter," Ali said in dismay as Genie lifted her back onto the bed. "How am I going to get to sleep?"

Genie picked up Ali's sparkly pink sunglasses, which lay on the desk. "No problem," she laughed. "I'll wear these."

She put the sunglasses on and climbed back into bed.

"But what about me?" Ali grumbled. She wasn't going to wear sunglasses at night! Besides, she didn't have any that would fit her.

"You could sleep under the quilt," Genie said, lifting it up.

"No, thanks," Ali said. "You might squash me. Besides, it's too hot!" Sighing, she climbed back to her place on the pillow and buried her face in it to block out the light. She was sure she was never going to get to sleep.

***

"Ali, hurry up. It's time for school. Ali!"

Ali woke at the sound of Little Genie's voice. She blinked and sat up, rubbing her eyes. She was still tired because it had taken her forever to fall asleep. Her heart sank as she realized that nothing had changed. She was still tiny, Genie still looked exactly like her, the lamp was still glowing brightly, and Ray was still asleep on his flying carpet.

Genie was standing in the middle of the bedroom, already dressed in jeans and a blue top. "Look," she announced, holding out her wrist. "There's still lots of sand to run through the hourglass. That means I'll have to go to school again today."

"Oh." Ali felt a bit upset. She had been looking forward to the special cooking class they had once a week. And Mrs. Jasmine was going to be reading students' stories to the class in language arts, and Ali didn't want to miss that.

"Do you want to come with me again?" Genie asked. "Yesterday was fun!"

Ali hesitated, then shook her head. "No, thanks. What if the sand ran through and we changed back in the middle of class?" She sighed. "Just put me on my desk and I'll find something to do."

Genie scooped Ali up and carried her over to the desk. Then she slung the backpack over her shoulder and opened the door. "Have a great day, Ali. See you!"

Ali listened to Genie run downstairs. She sat gloomily on the desk, swinging her legs. She was bored already. Ray was still asleep. There were some magazines and books on the desk, so Ali went over to see if she could find something to read.

The pile of books looked as big as paving slabs, and it was really difficult to pull the top one off the heap. It took Ali ages, and she was hot and breathless by the time she managed to open it. She began to read, but the print was so huge, it made her eyes hurt, and turning each page was a struggle. In the end, Ali gave up. She glanced at the clock. To her dismay, it was only halfway through the morning.

Ray turned over, mumbling in his sleep again. *"Now, I'll do the R-30 at a special price just for you, with go-faster fringes thrown in for nothing, can't-do better than that. . . ."*

"Is he ever going to wake up?" Ali wondered out loud. She felt a bit dizzy and her head hurt. It was probably because she hadn't had enough sleep last night.

Then she looked down at her hand. Her fingers were tingling. Was it her imagination, or were they getting *bigger*? Yes, they were! And that meant—

Ali leapt to her feet. She had to get off the desk! But it was too late. In seconds she shot right up to her full height. She had to duck to avoid hitting her head on the ceiling.

Pop! Ray, his flying carpet, and his sun-lamp disappeared.

Ali couldn't help feeling very relieved, even though she had liked Ray. "I'm back to normal!" she exclaimed. "All the sand must have run through Genie's hourglass."

She climbed down from the desk, feeling much happier. Now she could enjoy herself for the rest of the day and watch TV.

But a terrible thought suddenly struck her. If all the wishes were over and *she* was back to normal, then that meant Little Genie was back to normal too. And that meant Genie was somewhere at school, looking like Genie instead of Ali!

Chapter Ten
A Little Doughnut

"Nearly there!" Ali panted, running at full speed down the street toward Montgomery Elementary. She'd thrown on a pair of jeans and a dark blue top and dashed out of the house. Somehow she'd have to take Genie's place in the class without anyone noticing. Genie would be small again, so it should be easy for her to hide somewhere.

Ali raced across the playground and

was just about to run into school when the bell rang. A moment later, all the doors opened and everyone began to pour outside for recess. Ali's class was one of the first out. Tiffany and her friends appeared; then Mary came running out. She did a double take when she saw Ali.

"How did *you* get out here so fast?" she asked. "Honestly, Ali, you've been acting weird all morning!"

"I didn't feel well," Ali said quickly. "Mrs. Jasmine said I could come outside for some fresh air."

"Oh." Mary still looked puzzled. "You looked okay a few minutes ago." She stared at Ali's shirt. "Weren't you wearing a light blue shirt?"

Ali tried to laugh. "I guess the color just looks different in the sunlight," she said. "I—I think I need to go get a drink." She ran back inside, leaving Mary staring after her.

Hoping that none of the teachers would spot her, Ali dashed along the corridor, past an army of cleaning people mopping up the puddles in the hallway, and raced to the kitchen classroom.

The kitchen was empty. Cooling racks covered with chocolate chip cookies were lined up on the counters. A delicious smell lingered in the air.

Ali looked around frantically. "Genie!" she called softly. "It's me, Ali. Are you here?"

At first she didn't hear anything, but

then . . . was that a moan? It seemed to be coming from a canister of sugar!

Ali leaned across the counter and fished cautiously around inside the sugar canister. In a moment she pulled out a very sugary Genie! "Are you all right?" Ali cried, trying to dust her off. "What happened?"

"I was leaning across the counter when the wishes ran out." Genie sneezed, wiping sugar from her face. "When I shrank, I fell into the sugar! Luckily everyone was too busy tasting their cookies to notice."

"Let's get you cleaned up," Ali said, trying not to laugh. Genie looked like a little doughnut! She took Genie over to the sink and dabbed at her with a damp paper towel until all the sugar was off.

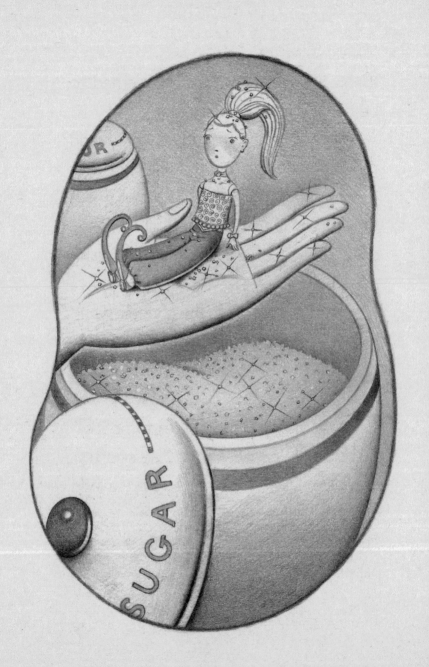

Genie was almost clean when the bell rang again for the end of recess. A moment later, there were footsteps in the corridor.

"Everyone's coming back to get their cookies," Ali whispered. "You'd better hide!" She picked Genie up and popped her into her pocket.

A second later, Mrs. Jasmine walked in with the class behind her. "Ali!" said the teacher, looking rather annoyed. "What are you doing in here?"

"I just wanted to check on my cookies, Mrs. Jasmine," Ali said. She could see that Mary was looking suspiciously at her again, so she grabbed the baking rack that held Genie's cookies. "Would anyone like to try one?"

Everyone crowded around. Not surprisingly, Tiffany and her friends pushed their way to the front and took the first cookies.

"I bet they're not as nice as mine," Tiffany said scornfully, taking the biggest cookie of all.

"Ali!" Genie tugged frantically at Ali's shirt.

"What's the matter?" Ali said under her breath. "The cookies look great!" Ali hoped that if the cookies were yummy enough, Tiffany might just forget about Genie making her look stupid on the basketball court.

"I'm not sure Tiffany's going to like those cookies much," Genie confessed as Tiffany took a big bite. "I made the cookies exactly the way genies like them—with extra-hot pepper!"

Ali watched in horror as her class-mates began to cough, their eyes watering. She turned her back on them and locked eyes with Little Genie.

"Turn the hourglass upside down!" Ali said urgently as Tiffany pushed past her to get a glass of water. "I need my next set of wishes to start right now!"

Read more about the adventures of
Ali and Little Genie in
Little Genie: *A Puff of Pink*!

Ali wanted to liven up her room a bit.
Add some color. But Little Genie has mixed
up her magic—and now everything Ali
touches turns pink! Her bedspread, her T-shirt,
her backpack—and the uniforms of the
entire soccer team!
Will Ali have to think pink forever?